BUT MARTIN!

JUNE COUNSEL

Pictures by Carolyn Dinan

PICTURE CORGI BOOKS

That first morning back at school

Lee's lips turned down
Lloyd's head hung down
Billy's brows drew down
And Angela's tears fell down

but that was before they found

MARTIN!

Lee's face was smooth and golden
Lloyd's face was round and brown

Billy's face was square and red
And Angela's face was long and white

but Martin's face was

GREEN!

Lee's hair was black and silky
Lloyd's hair was black and bouncy

Billy's hair was red and spiky
And Angela's hair was fair and floaty

but Martin's hair

WASN'T THERE!

(he just had these)

When they saw him

Lee giggled
Lloyd shouted

Billy whistled
and Angela gasped

but Martin

BLEEPED!

Then they began to play.

Lloyd jumped

Lee skipped

Billy chased

and Angela cartwheeled

but Martin

FLOATED!

The bell rang and
Lee stood still
Lloyd stopped dead
Billy wobbled

and Angela froze

but Martin

VANISHED!

When they got to their classroom
    Lee
    Lloyd
    Billy
    and Angela

came through
the door

but Martin
came through the

WALL!

Now

Lee knew a little
Lloyd knew a lot
Billy knew a bit
and Angela knew most things
(so she thought)

but Martin knew

EVERYTHING!

When they had maths
   Lee did Take-Aways
   Lloyd did Adds
   Billy did Matching
   and Angela did
     Take-Away-You-Can'ts!

But Martin did

THE ANSWERS IN HIS HEAD!

and he showed them what to do

and they all got it right!

When they had English
Lee spelt *they* with an *a*
Lloyd spelt *was* with an *oz*

Billy got *d* the wrong way round
and Angela left *n* out of *went*

but Martin spelt

PEOPLE

with a *p* and an *e*
and an *o* and a *p*
and an *l* and an *e*
which is right!

and he taught them all how to spell
and they never forgot!

When school ended

Lee went home in her Mum's new car
Lloyd went home on his battered old bike

Billy went home in the three thirty bus
and Angela walked home on her own
two feet

but Martin went home in his

SAUCER!

BUT MARTIN!
A PICTURE CORGI BOOK : 0 552 523127

First published in Great Britain by Faber and Faber Ltd in 1984

PRINTING HISTORY
Picture Corgi edition published 1986

16 18 20 19 17 15

Picture Corgi Books are published by Transworld Publishers,
61-63 Uxbridge Road, London W5 5SA,
a division of The Random House Group Ltd.

Printed in Belgium